Episode 9

HBO max

Let's *Stick* Together

CHANDRA CRAWFORD

for Elle —
Hope you enjoy!
Chandra

Editor: Sassie Lewis
Illustrator: Willsin Rowe
Formatted by: JC Clarke, The Graphics Shed

18+ DUE TO SEXUAL CONTENT.

From high school frenemies to true love.
It could happen. Couldn't it?

Back in high school, bad boy Wade Davies had a huge crush on Eva-Marie Robinson. She was perfecta curvy, copper-skinned princess who mesmerized him with her golden eyes. She was also his brother's girlfriend, and off-limits. After the night that changed his life forever, Wade made sure the princess stayed far away from him.

Eva-Marie has wanted Wade since high since high school, but her relationship with his younger brother, Scott, makes anything between them an impossibility. Add to that, he can't stand to be around her, and it equals zero chances she can have the one guy she craves.

Fifteen years later, Wade is the drummer for The Bladesmiths, his brother Scott's uber-successful band. They reconnect, and have the potential for an explosive love that rocks both their worlds. But, new obstacles may put and end to things before they've begun, and leave Wade and Eva-Marie irreconcilable enemies.

CHAPTER
1

2003- 18 YEARS OLD

She was here again. The private school princess that hung out with his little brother was back. She came over after school almost every day now. There were other kids, too, sometimes, but Wade barely knew who they were. Something about her drew his attention whenever she was around. It wasn't just her looks. She was beautiful, but beautiful girls were after him all the time. His reputation as a bad boy had made its way around the high school. Being hauled in by the cops a couple of times, even though he was innocent, had done wonders for his social life. Girls from every clique were ready to do almost anything to be his. Even a couple of the teachers had stealthily hit on him. The whole situation was ridiculous, but it hadn't kept him from seizing a few opportunities.

But the young princess was out of his league. In all his eighteen years, Wade had never seen anyone like her before. She was tall, almost as tall as his own six feet. He'd barely have to hold his head down to kiss her. She'd fill up his arms just right. All soft curves and cushiony handfuls. And the way she walked- like she owned the universe, her back straight and head so high you could practically see the crown. Though Wade normally went for the slim, cheerleader types, the sway of this girl's wider hips and round ass had him practically hypnotized. She could be walking through the halls at school carrying her books and still manage to look like a ballerina. Shit.

Grimacing at the direction his thought had taken, Wade bent to look in the refrigerator, seeking a distraction. Nothing interesting in there, except his father's weird imported beer. Snagging one, he popped the top and took a deep swig before heading down the hall to his own room. The last thing he wanted to do was bump into the princess. He immediately became a tongue-tied dork, barely able to grunt hi, then scowling at her to cover his embarrassment.

Walking past Scott's room, a flash of movement caught his eye through a crack where the door wasn't fully closed. He paused, and saw a shiny red object floated to the floor, landing almost squarely in his line of vision. A red, silky tank top. Exactly like the one the princess had been wearing. Wade's gaze flew to the sliver of mirror he could see without hesitation.

They were lying on Scott's bed, kissing. His jeans clad leg was thrown across hers, her bare toes pressed against his sock. He was shirtless, leaning over her. She still wore a red bra that matched her missing tank. As Wade watched, his brother ran his hand up the smooth, coppery skin of her belly, moving steadily closer to the red lace-covered promised land.

Stalking back toward the kitchen, Wade turned up the beer bottle, chugging the remainder of the contents and tossing the empty before slamming out the back door. Jumping into his halfway restored classic hot rod, he roared down the driveway. Burning rubber, he sped away toward the drive-in theater where he and his friends usually hung out after dark.

He pulled into their regular spot near screen four, and his buddies immediately surrounded the car, climbing in once he put the top down, and tossing him a beer. Wade guzzled that one down, ate a handful of popcorn from somebody's bag, and grabbed another can. Maybe if he drank enough, he could blot out the memory of the princess' beautiful brown skin with his brother's hands all over it. Or how eaten up with jealousy he was because Scott was the one who got to kiss her. And who knows what the fuck else he was doing to her by now.

Popping the top on the next brew, he drank deeply.

By the end of the double feature, Wade was seeing in multiples and slurring his words. He couldn't remember either of the two movies, but he hadn't forgotten the red bra, or how angry he was that Scott was touching it. He was going home right now and putting a stop to that shit. He fumbled for the keys, but they kept moving away from his grasp.

"Dude, you're drunk. I'll drive."

That was Jeremy. Cool. He didn't trust anyone with his car. She was his baby. But he had to go save the princess. At least Jeremy's dad was a cop. If they got pulled over, he could get them out of trouble. Jeremy was always getting out of trouble. His dad seemed determined to send Wade up the river, though.

After sliding into the passenger seat, Wade finally got the seatbelt buckled, then laid back to rest for a moment. He didn't feel so hot, and his mouth tasted like stale beer and burnt popcorn. He must have nodded off. A sharp yank on his shoulder woke him up. He blinked rapidly, trying to focus through the pain in his head and the churning in his stomach. His beloved hot rod was parked dangerously close to a tree. Jeremy was no longer in the driver's seat, but there was a smear of blood on the steering wheel. It was lit up in the glow of the lights from the police car behind him.

"Finally got'cha," Wade heard as Jeremy's father, Officer Fargas, pulled him roughly from the wreckage and slapped on a pair of handcuffs.

As he was hustled to the police car, Wade passed by Jeremy, who was sitting on the ground in a puddle of his own barf, holding his bloody head. He looked as bad as Wade felt. But that didn't let him off the hook for wrecking his baby. They would get it all sorted out at the police station.

****

2005- 20 YEARS OLD

A year and a half in jail for drunk driving. Innocent. Destruction of property. Innocent.

And underage drinking. Guilty. Thanks to the quick thinking, and even faster talking, of Officer Fargas, his own son was never involved. Even Wade's parents believed he was guilty of all the charges. After all, who takes the word of a sloppy drunk teenager over the long arm of the law? Only Scott knew his big brother was innocent. He was the one person who took it on faith that none of what happened was his fault, and that he hadn't even been driving the car. And the only one who could never know why Wade had gotten so drunk in the first place.

Still, here he was. Home just in time to attend his little brother's graduation. Wade was proud of Scott. While he'd been locked up, Scott's band had been posting their rehearsals online. They'd gone from a little garage band to an internet sensation, garnering the kind of attention that eventually turned into a recording contract. In a few days, Scott would be off to Hollywood to become the star he deserved to be. Meanwhile, Wade had a jailhouse G. E. D. and certifications in auto mechanics and auto body repair. He wasn't bitter. At least not towards Scott and his success. But the urge to wonder "what if" was strong sometimes.

"Scott Davies." Wade stood and clapped, whistling loudly as his brother strolled across the stage and received his diploma. The applause was thunderous. Everyone was happy for the boy who was going to be famous. Scott gave an embarrassed little wave and hurried to his seat.

The rest of the names were just background noise while Wade daydreamed about fixing the hot rod and getting it back on the road. It wouldn't take much. The door and the rear quarter panel had taken most of the impact. The frame was still solid. He'd have to check the rear suspension for damage. It was great that his parents had kept it for him all this time. They knew how much he loved that car.

"Eva-Marie Robinson."

The name broke through his daydream. He watched the princess walk gracefully across the stage, checking out everything from her hairstyle to her strappy high heels. She appeared to be lit from within, her skin glowing golden under the spotlights. He'd thought of her every single day, but seeing her now, all grown up and womanly, was a shock to the system. Wade clapped automatically along with the audience, but he could barely swallow around the lump in his throat.

Eva-Marie turned and waved to her family, and her gaze met his as it swept the crowd. She hesitated, staring for a second like a deer in headlights. Then she was shaking the principal's hand, and the moment was gone.

Later, in the reception area, all the students and parents were gathered, chatting about their plans for the future, taking pictures, and saying their goodbyes. Wade leaned against a wall, sipping terrible punch and waiting for the crowd around his brother to thin out. As the other kids slowly drifted away from him, the princess stepped to Scott. Speaking quietly for a minute, they laughed, then embraced each other. As they hugged, Eva-Marie's gaze once again sought him out. She raised a hand in a shy wave, as if she

9

was unsure whether her greeting would be welcome. He returned it with a half-hearted smile and a salute with the nasty punch. It was the best he could do while she was in Scott's arms. Tossing the cup into the nearest trash can, he walked away.

After dinner, Wade drove Scott to the airport at his request.

"You sure you don't want to come with me?" Scott looked worried about him.

"Nah, man," he assured him. "Nothing for me to do in L.A. I'll be fine here."

"You're positive? I can always request you as my drummer." Scott nudged Wade with his elbow, making him laugh.

"Hah. Playing in the basement is one thing. Being in your band is something else. Besides, I like working with cars. Old man Hunsaker is going to show me how to supercharge the Corvette after I get it fixed."

"Sweet. Call me if you change your mind."

Wade hugged his little brother tightly, happy for him, but sad to see him go.

"Good things, man," he told Scott.
"You too, bro. Nothing but."

CHAPTER 2

2014

The call came at six a.m., Memphis time.

"Hey, bro. Did I wake you?"

"Only half an hour before my alarm." Wade was instantly alert. "What's up?"

"My drummer. Dude's got some heavy drug problems. We can't cover for him any more. The record label is sending him to rehab, but either way, they're pulling him out of the band."

"And you're calling me because...?" Wade

had an inkling where this conversation was going, and Scott was beating a dead horse.

"I need a drummer. You're elected."

"Hell no." Wade rubbed his hand over his face, then turned on the bedside lamp. "You know I'm not a professional."

"No matter," Scott insisted. "You're still the best drummer I know. I need someone I can trust."

"Trust is great," Wade argued, "but it won't get me through a tour. It's been years since I've played on a regular basis."

"Bullshit." Scott snorted the way he did when he was being a smartass. "I know you still play with the radio to keep your skills up."

"Yeah. So?" Wade didn't like where this was going.

"So, do you ever play to our tracks?"

Caught, Wade said nothing. Instead, he rolled out of bed and shuffled to the kitchen to start the coffee pot.

Scott laughed.

"You already know all the beats then, right?"

13

His teasing tone became laughter at Wade's noncommittal grunt. "A couple of rehearsals and you'll be fine. I have faith in you, big brother."

Trying one final tactic, Wade reminded Scott, "I have a business to run."

For the last six years, Wade had been the owner of the garage he'd renamed Boost Turtle Custom Cars. Mr. Hunsaker, after a serious health scare and some not-so-subtle threats from his wife, decided to retire. Since Mrs. Hunsaker was anxious to become the grand dame of Boca Raton, they'd sold him the business for a ridiculously low price, and moved to sunny Florida. They attributed their asking price to sweat equity, saying Wade was the reason they could afford their dream retirement. His skills and the clients he'd brought in for custom upgrades had completely revitalized the business. For his own part, Wade was thankful every day that Mr. Hunsaker had taken a chance on him. The shop was proof that he'd been worth it.

"Yeah, I know." The teasing tone was gone from Scott's voice. "And I know how much it means to you. But BJ and Chad are the best. They've taken care of your garage like it was their own whenever you've come for visits before. I'm sure they will again. We're talking a couple of months. Just until the tour is over and we can audition new drummers. Please, bro, do this for me."

He was sunk. Scott had never really asked him for anything. Not even when they were kids. Now, Scott needed him. He'd even said please. Of course, Wade wouldn't let his brother down. He couldn't.

Back when the bank said he'd needed collateral for his loan to buy the shop, Scott volunteered to cosign the papers without hesitation. Hell, he'd offered to give him the money outright, but Wade refused, preferring to pay his own way. And, of course, Wade had never forgotten that Scott and the Hunsakers were the only ones who'd believed him when he swore he'd been set up. That meant more to him than anything else.

Absentmindedly taking a sip of coffee, he

sputtered, then added sugar and cream. Leaning against the counter, he took another sip, then sighed deeply.

"I'll need a few days to make arrangements." Being a good brother was damned inconvenient.

"You have twenty-four hours." Scott was brusque, but the relief in his voice was clear. "I'll send you a plane ticket. I really appreciate this, Wade."

"Sure. No problem." The sarcasm was thick enough to spread on toast.

Scott's laughter roared in his ears until the line went dead.

****

By the time Wade's plane landed in Los Angeles, the announcement had already been made that he was joining The Bladesmiths as their new drummer. There were so many calls and texts coming through his phone, he'd turned it off mid-flight. Other than the message from Scott that said, 'Meet you at the airport. Get ready,' none of the rest of them interested him

16

anyway.

Scott waited just beyond the security gate with several bodyguards. He wore sunglasses and a baseball cap, but Wade would know him anywhere. Apparently, at least half of Los Angeles did, too. Every t.v. show in the state of California had a camera crew there. The flashing lights and shouted questions came at him like the rapid fire from an automatic weapon. When he could actually hear a question through the cacophony, it was always pertaining to his relationship status or his time incarcerated. The flight had only taken a few hours. These people worked fast. He'd have to remember that. Scowling, he said nothing.

Scott moved from behind the barrier of his security detail, coming to embrace him warmly. Taking Wade's baggage claim tickets, he handed them to a bodyguard, who silently melted away into the crowd of reporters.

Wade felt Scott's arm land across his shoulders, then he was moving toward the exit, surrounded by the fortress of stone-faced guards.

Though it probably appeared to everyone else that Scott was simply happy to see his brother, especially with the overly bright grin he wore, Wade was subtly being herded through the crowd by the altering pressure of Scott's arm and hand. It was like being led in strange dance, but instead he was guided among the press of bodies much quicker and easier than he'd thought possible.

Outside, however, was chaos. The same source that told fans he'd be flying in today had also informed The Bladesmiths' fans that Scott would be there to meet him. A million screams erupted on cue as they stepped from the building into the sunshine. Airport and metro police struggled to maintain the barricades they'd set up to hold back the masses of people gathered there. An ocean of cellphones recorded their every move. Holy hell! Was this what his life about to become?

In all the times he'd traveled to meet Scott on tour or visit him during his downtime, this was something he'd been shielded from. When Wade traveled to wherever his brother was staying, they were practically alone just hanging out the entire time they were together, other than when he was on stage. This was madness. Far crazier in person than anything he'd seen on t.v. Celebrities had to be nuts to deal with this type of thing all the time.

Scott, appearing unfazed, started blowing kisses to the multitude of fans. But behind his hand, Wade heard him say, "Truck number two. Move. Move. Move." The security team was subtle, but they moved with military precision.

Quickening his steps, Wade slipped past the guard into the open door of the SUV, closely followed by Scott. The door slammed shut, and they were immediately in motion. One of the men in front confirmed they were okay, then raised the partition between the seats to give them some privacy.

"It's like that all the time?" He knew Scott was uber famous, but that was some wild shit he'd just witnessed. After all, it was his brother, not the second coming of Kurt Cobain.

"Yeah." Scott shrugged, the huge grin gone. "You get used to it. Fans are why you have a career in the first place. Always be nice to them."

"Hey, you're the superstar. I'm just the drummer. And a temporary one at that."

Scott waved away his words like they were so much nonsense.

"You're in The Bladesmiths. And my brother," he explained. "You'll probably get as much attention as I do. You handled that well. Good strategy, the silence. Build the mystery. Let them wonder about you."

Hah. Wade was sure he'd just bought his own ticket to the Rock Group Funny Farm. *Fine. If having nothing to say was what worked for him, he had no problem making it a habit.*

CHAPTER 3

2018

Wade reached in the refrigerator and snagged one of his father's weird imported beers. Thirty-three years old and he was still doing that. He'd figured out years ago that his Dad bought extras to share, but he liked to fuss about the "thefts" of his favorite beer. Tonight, his parents were just happy to see him and Scott. After four years, most of it spent on the road with The Bladesmiths, he was glad to be home for more than a couple of days. For the moment, they had a few months free, with the upcoming concert on Beale Street being the only exception. Scott said he was planning use the time to write some new music, and Wade was anxious to get back home to privacy, his classic car, and Boost Turtle.

BJ and Chad had been wonderful while he was off playing rock star. They'd kept the shop running smoothly, and their excellent work brought in so many new customers they were taking jobs by appointment only. The fact that The Bladesmiths' drummer owned the business and did custom work himself hadn't hurt their reputation any, either. Several other celebrities sent him messages saying how pleased they were with the work his shop had done. The guys had more than earned all the raises they'd been given. Recently, he'd let them buy into the business as well. Whenever he was ready for his own "Boca" to retire to, they could step in and have it all, if they wanted.

In the meantime, the garage was his haven.

He couldn't wait to get back to it, and just being a regular guy. In the morning, he planned to give his condo a once-over, then get good and dirty working on his baby, the same 1962 red Corvette Convertible he'd had in high school.

Going over to his parents' back door, Wade stared out into the darkness. She was on his mind again. To be honest, she was never far from it. More so when he was in Memphis, and almost constantly when he was in this house. Here, the red tank top hitting the floor and the red bra were etched into his memory so vividly, it all could have happened yesterday.

Since Scott and Eva-Marie were still good friends, they still spoke on the phone and social media on a regular basis. She would tell Scott to say hello to him for her all the time. Though he played it cool and casual, his heart always fluttered a little when she remembered him. Shame usually followed. She was still his brother's girl, even though they hadn't been together in years. He'd never disrespect Scott by creating such an awkward situation.

Pushing through the screen door, Wade stepped out into the night. Beer and crickets could keep him company until he was done dwelling on her.

****

Eva-Marie hugged Scott, then his parents. She was so happy to see them all again. This house had been like her second home when she was a teenager. After moving to America and Memphis at sixteen, she'd been shy and slow to make friends. Scott -intrigued by her accent, he said- approached her after school one day, peppering her with questions about growing up in Australia, the embassy in Canberra, and her father, the diplomat. She'd been amused, laughing at him trying to mimic her speech, and flattered that the cutest and most popular boy in school found her interesting.

Over the next few days, Scott had walked her to class, grilling her like a rookie cop. His friends, apparently used to him being more of the strong, silent type, assumed his interest in the new girl was more than friendly. Scott, confiding to her his disinterest in most of the girls at school competing for his attention, came up with the idea to let them think so. It was the perfect solution, allowing them to avoid uncomfortable social confrontations with other boys and girls, and explore their budding friendship in private.

Fifteen years later, they were still the best of friends. They'd studied together, partied together, even traveled together. Except for the one ill-fated attempt at romance back in high school, they were as close as they'd always been. Mrs. Davies hugged her tightly, pulling Eva-Marie down to sit on the sofa beside her.

"Tell me what you've been doing since the last time we saw you, honey. I know you've been traveling a lot. I want to hear all about it."

Half an hour later, she and the Davies family were all caught up. The parents were retired for the night after additional hugs and promises to visit more often. Then she and Scott were alone. After joking around for a bit, he smiled at her the way he always did when he knew she was stalling.

"So what's up with you?" she goaded him.

Scott leaned back in his chair, stretching his long legs out and crossing them at the ankles.

"I think it's more interesting to talk about what's up with you," he responded, smirking.

"Nothing's up with me. You know that." Eva-Marie plucked at imaginary lint on her pants and gave Scott an innocent smile.

"Hah."

"Shut up."

He grinned.

She picked up the closest thing to her, a cardboard coaster, and threw it, smacking him squarely in the forehead. They both collapsed in fits of laughter, trying to be quiet so they didn't disturb his parents, the same way they'd done so many nights as teens.

"Go ahead and ask," Scott teased, still smiling. "You know you want to."

"No."

"I'm not volunteering any information."

"Bastard." Eva-Marie hated when Scott tortured her like this. It was pure evil.

He chuckled and pushed her foot with the toe of his boot.

"Come on," he insisted. "Do it."

"Fine." She huffed and stuck her tongue out at him. "How is your brother?"

"Now, was that so hard?"

She grimaced. "You have no idea."

Scott leaned forward and patted Eva-Marie on the thigh. She knew he was trying to be helpful, but her stomach was full of butterflies.

"He's in the kitchen. I heard him come inside a minute ago. Why don't you go ask him?"

"Oh no." Eva-Marie looked horrified. "I couldn't do that. I don't think I've ever said more than hello to him because he was always kind of mean to me. I've told you I don't think he likes me much. Besides, I'll freeze up. I won't know what to say."

"And I told you he likes you just fine. You speak to foreign delegations all the time. You can talk to him. He's just a guy. And you're an intelligent, beautiful woman. Plus, you're sexy as hell. If he's smart, he'll wrap himself around your little finger and stay there."

She laughed. "You're silly."

"I'm right."

Scott stood up, and she allowed him to pull her to her feet. He kept pulling until they were in the hallway, and she didn't resist even though her nerves were tied in knots.

"I'm going to bed," he told her. "Call me tomorrow and tell me how it turns out."

Eva-Marie felt Scott kiss her cheek and push her gently toward the kitchen, but her mind was filled with thoughts of what she would say to Wade when she got there. Willing her feet to keep moving, she gave herself a pep talk. *He is right. It's now or never. It's been much too long already. What's the worst that could happen? He doesn't date chubby girls? He doesn't date black chicks? He doesn't like me? Either way, his loss. Like Scott said, I'm great. OR, I could completely humiliate myself, which would be bad. So very bad.*

Turning around, intending to quietly sneak out before Wade noticed her, she ran face first into Scott, who had followed her.

"Chicken," he whispered, and headed her back toward the kitchen. "Get in there and do your thing." He stepped back and crossed his arms, leaning against the wall, letting her know he wasn't leaving until she was inside the other room.

Damn him. He's going to stay here until I give in and talk to Wade. Bastard. He's going to pay later. From the way he was smirking at her, he already knew it. Rolling her eyes at Scott, she took a deep breath and strode off to spin the proverbial wheel of fortune.

Wade was bent over, rooting around in the refrigerator. Her gaze involuntarily zoomed in on his ass, and how perfectly it filled the black jeans which were molded to it. They showcased his taut cheeks superbly, and hugged the muscles in his thighs as he moved to reach for something, then stood up. Busy watching the rippling and flexing beneath the denim, it didn't click fully that not only was she still staring, but she was looking at his crotch now. The view there was just as impressive. *Damn.*

The soft snick of the beer bottle opening startled her. When she raised her eyes to his, it was to find him looking as unsettled as she was. *Okay. Deep breath.*

"Hello, Wade." She stepped to the island and slid onto a stool. At the moment, she couldn't trust her knees not to give out. "How have you been?"

"Good."

"Good," she repeated nervously.

Wade set the beer on the counter and slid his hands into his pockets, stretching the sexy jeans even tighter across his hips and thighs and, um, package. Her mind stuttered as she watched.

"So, um, it's great to see you. I looked for you a couple of times when I came home, but we never seem to be here at the same time. Until now."

He seemed puzzled. "Why?"

"To say hi. To see you. Since we practically grew up together, I thought that would be okay. Was I wrong?"

"No," he replied quickly, "that's fine."

"I've been keeping up with your career. With the band, I mean. Not everyone can say their besties are celebrities." She smiled at him. "I made it to a couple of shows, but that was a while ago, before you joined them."

Wade said nothing. He raised his beer and took a long drink without ever breaking eye contact with Eva-Marie, making her squirm in her seat. But, she'd started down this path now. She was determined to see it through.

"Anyway, I have to go now. I have an early meeting. But why don't we get together later and have coffee or something?"

His expression hardened for some reason, reminding her of when they were younger. He never smiled then, either. Just walked around scowling at everyone. The most terrifyingly gorgeous boy in school. He took her breath away, and absolutely scared her to death back then. He still did now.

"Coffee with me?" He gave a sarcastic snort. "What for? Didn't you come here to get with my brother? Sorry, I can't help you with that."

31

What. The. Hell. Eva-Marie bristled in response to Wade's nasty tone. *Who does he think he is, speaking to me like that?* She stood, drawing herself up to her full height. *I'm not taking that crap, I don't care who he is.*

"Well, I hate to disappoint you, Wade, but no, I'm not here to *get with* your brother. We're friends. We've always been friends. We wanted to see each other, so I came to visit. Friends do that. And for future reference, if I wanted to get with anyone, I would do so. And it wouldn't require any assistance. I have no issues in that area. I thoroughly resent being spoken to like some groupie."

Looking shocked by her outburst, Wade set his bottle down on the counter. He started to say something, then cleared his throat and tried again.

"That was rude of me. Sorry." His dark, serious eyes studied her again, this time more thoughtfully, it seemed.

"Apology accepted. So, coffee, yes?"

He nodded.

Fishing around in her purse, Eva-Marie located a business card and a pen. After scribbling her home and cellphone numbers on the back, she slid it across the island to Wade.

"See you soon." She spoke quietly, back to her usual self after her brief flare of temper earlier. "Have a good night."

Eva-Marie was sure she could feel his stare burning into her skin as she walked away.

CHAPTER
4

Wade sat in his car watching the café across the street. From his position, he could see Eva-Marie sitting inside, waiting for him. He'd arrived fifteen minutes early to give himself time to chill a bit before she got there. She must have had the same idea, because she was already there when he drove up. In the time he'd been observing her, Eva-Marie must have checked her watch at least twice, fiddled with her hair, and refreshed her lipstick. The princess was getting impatient, perhaps? Well, he had a few more minutes. She could wait.

He'd thought more than once about calling off this date. Was still thinking of backing out. What the hell was he doing with *her*? They were as opposite as two people could be. As far as he knew, they had nothing in common. At all. What the fuck were they going to talk about, other than Scott?

Just then, she looked through the window, straight at him. She smiled shyly, and gave a little wave. *Damn, she was beautiful.* Wade got out of his car and walked toward the coffee shop in a daze, like he was being called by a siren and couldn't resist her. Before he knew what was happening, he was standing beside the table where she was sitting.

"Hi, Wade. I'm so glad you could make it."

She sounded genuine, and her smile looked sincere. But why would the princess be so happy to see him? He was nobody to her.

"Hey, Eva-Marie." He sat down across from her, trying not to notice their knees touching under the table. She apparently did, though. She moved so her legs stretched between his, and he could extend his long limbs beside hers.

"There. Hopefully, that's more comfortable for you. These tiny little spaces are not built for two tall people. I wanted a booth, but..." She fluttered her hand in the direction of all the booths, which were occupied.

"No problem. This is fine." Wade was still wondering why he bothered to show up. This was not his scene at all.

"I love your car. You've done all the work yourself, yes? Scott's told me about your garage, and the restorations you do. I'm not surprised. I remember how awesome your car was when we were teenagers."

"Thanks." Wade relaxed with her compliments, and the familiar direction of the conversation. "I've done a lot of work on it, but the restoration is still in progress." He filled her in on more of the details as they drank their coffee and munched on pastries, happily surprised that she seemed to actually be interested in talking shop with him.

"What about you?" he asked, turning the conversation around. "You're running your parents' foundation now, right?"

"Yes. I left the politics to Dad and my brother. I was never interested in all that. They spend most of their time in Washington, D.C. I live here and run the Robinson Foundation. That is, when I'm not globetrotting to raise or distribute funds."

She chattered on about the children she'd met and helped through her work, and Wade watched her, fascinated. He could tell she loved what she did. Her eyes, a warm shade of golden brown, sparkled as she spoke. She talked with her hands, waving them gracefully around, animating her words. She'd always done that. It was one of the things about her he found so charming. Then again, he was drawn to everything about Eva-Marie, from the reddish-brown curls that hung to her shoulders, to the burnished copper of her skin, to the husky honey of her voice that stubbornly held on to a slight trace of Australia.

She was beauty and class, and he was an ex-con who got fifteen minutes of fame riding his little brother's coattails.

And about Scott, why wasn't she here with him instead? Scott was the one she had history with, so what exactly did she want from Wade? He couldn't figure her out. She was definitely flirting with him. She'd moved her legs under the table several times to make sure they remained in contact with his. But no matter how much he enjoyed her company, nothing could come of it anyway. With his background, he didn't exactly fit into Eva-Marie's world. A relationship with him could potentially damage her reputation. Maybe her brother's as well, since he was running for office. Women with her kind of breeding weren't the type for temporary flings. To avoid causing her any scandal, he'd better keep his distance.

When the check came, he reached for it, but Eva-Marie snatched it up before he could touch it. He tried to steal it away when she was digging through her purse, but she caught him at it and smacked his hand.

"My treat. I invited you."

"A gentleman pays when he's out with a beautiful lady." She beamed at his words, but held on to the slip of paper.

"While I appreciate your chivalry, and the compliment, I never asked you to be a gentleman." She winked at him. "Remember that. It might come in handy."

The following day, Wade was in his office ordering parts for a 1950 Studebaker Commander Convertible he was working on, along with some for his own Corvette. Whenever he was home, he liked to spend time on the Vette. Doing the restorations himself helped him focus and clear his mind. He could zone out and just concentrate on his hands, and the work they were doing. Necessary now, since his thoughts were filled with Eva-Marie. On tour, he'd done the same thing playing his drums. As long as his hands were busy, he could control how much time she spent inside his head.

"Yo, boss," he heard BJ call out. "You've got

company."

Wade walked into the waiting area, surprised to see Eva-Marie there. She looked spectacular, as always, in a snug blue tee shirt, expensive-looking jeans that molded to her shapely curves like cling wrap, and sparkly sandals. Even when she dressed down, she looked like a princess, just like she did in high school.

"Hey," he managed to croak out, finally. "Come on in and have a seat."

He ushered her into his office, unsuccessfully trying to ignore Chad and BJ making wild gestures out of Eva-Marie's sight. BJ drew an hourglass shape in the air, then tossed his long dreadlocks, mimicking Eva-Marie's sexy hair flip, which she must have done while she waited for him. BJ mouthed "wow" to Wade, giving him the thumbs up. Chad was pantomiming breasts and booty, uttering a low wolf whistle Wade hoped she couldn't hear. He rolled his eyes at their immature behavior, then flipped them off. Stepping into his office behind Eva-Marie, he shut the door, hesitated, then lowered the blinds as well.

As he walked around his desk, she fingered the small parts and paperwork near the edge. Dropping into his chair, he watched her carefully slide everything a few inches to the side, then settle herself on the desktop.

"Whoa." He took her hands and attempted to pull her off the dirty surface. "You shouldn't sit there. You'll mess up your expensive clothes."

She giggled charmingly, and slid her hands around his to flip his palms up. Looking down, he saw his own hands smudged with motor oil, his fingernails caked with grime. He'd already left matching smudges on her skin.

"Oh, shit." He grabbed a shop towel and scrubbed at her hands. "I'm sorry. I'm probably the dirtiest thing in here. You shouldn't be in this mess at all, princess."

She took the towel away from Wade and tossed it aside. He watched it flutter to the floor, then met her eyes, his own full of questions. She reached for his hands once more, holding them tightly in hers when he tried to pull away.

"Mechanics come with dirt and oil, yes?" she asked softly, with a lilt of Canberra in her husky voice.

He nodded.

"Then why should I expect anything else when I'm consorting with a mechanic?"

Wade laughed. He couldn't help it. She was so damned cute.

"Consorting? That's funny. Is that what we're doing?"

Eva-Marie slid from the desk onto his lap and placed his hands, which she still held, on her waist. Wiggling around to get comfortable, she ground her soft, bubble butt against him, causing an instant erection. Wrapping her arms around his neck, she pressed her lips to his.

That was all Wade could take. He kissed Eva-Marie like he'd been desperate to do since high school. A deep, soul-searching kiss that had her melting in his arms. She moaned against his lips, and he pressed hers open, exploring her mouth, trying to memorize everything. How each millimeter of her tasted. Which touches of his tongue made her groan and squirm. How she strained against his body, her fingers sifting through his hair, but her hold on him firm, as if she wanted even more.

Wade ran his hand across her hip and trailed it down to her ass, where he squeezed lightly. Sliding his other arm around her waist, he pulled her closer, rocking his hips slightly to rub his throbbing cock against the plush heat of her fantastic ass.

Eva-Marie moaned again, loudly this time. Loud enough to startle them both. They broke apart, his breathing hard and heavy. She trembled in his arms, her chest heaving as quickly as his own.

Meeting her wide-eyed gaze, he saw the questions reflected there, along with the desire. Attempting to reassure her, and maybe himself as well, he cuddled her closer, bending to rest his forehead against hers. The longing he felt was more than a match for hers. But his heart was involved. If he was going to risk it, he needed to be damned sure it was worth it, and that he could take the punishment.

"So, this is consorting?" His voice was still thick with lust.

Eva-Marie snuggled into Wade's embrace.

"Yes." She caressed his cheek, and lowered her head to rest on his chest. "That's exactly what this is."

****

Back in her car, Eva-Marie heaved a huge sigh of relief. She was so glad she'd finally taken Scott's advice and made the first move with Wade. She knew for certain from the coffee date that he was attracted to her, but for some unknown reason, he seemed determined to keep her at arm's length.

It had been all she could manage to choke down her nervousness and sit on his lap. When he hardened beneath her almost right away, she could have jumped up and cheered. Instead, she took a chance, and kissed him.

It turned out to be the best decision she'd made. He kissed her back with enough passion to scorch her lips. He had her moaning like they were actually having sex, just from his kisses. She might not be able to handle getting him naked if he could break her down like that while she was still fully clothed. Her legs still felt a little weak. Damn, he had some wicked talent in those lips.

She had to get a grip, though. She'd let him know she wanted him. He didn't need to know just how deeply she was under his spell. Wade had always been the most effortlessly sexy man she'd ever seen. Even as a teen, he'd been able to melt her with just a look. Unfortunately for her, most of the looks he cast in her direction were less than friendly. Scott assured her that Wade had never disliked her, but she wasn't so sure. As recently as a few days ago in his parents' kitchen, he'd been downright rude.

No matter how mutual their attraction, something about her still seemed to rub him the wrong way. She wished he'd just come out and say whatever it was, so they could get past it. She'd waited so long to be with him, and wanted this so much. The thought that she could lose

45

everything for some unknown reason when it was finally within reach was unbearable.

Hopefully, he was as ready as she was to see what could happen between them. Hanging on to that thought, she drove home.

****

Wade locked the garage doors and chuckled to himself. Chad and BJ had been ribbing him about Eva-Marie since she'd left. What was her name? Where had he been hiding her? Did she have any sisters? They were hilarious. It progressed to them sneaking up behind him quoting the lyrics to dirty rap songs. Assholes. He'd really missed them while he was on the road. Today, though, he'd threatened to fire them if they didn't fuck off. Which, of course, only made them worse. Still smiling, he mounted the stairs to his apartment above the shop.

After having a shower and dinner, Wade was still antsy. There was nothing on television, and he couldn't find a book that held his attention. As usual, he was thinking of Eva-Marie. After that kiss, her interest in him was pretty clear. He kept telling himself not to question his good fortune, but the thought of being a substitute for his brother still made him uneasy.

Cranking up some music, he sat down at his drums and played. By the fifth song, he was sweating like the stage lights were shining on him. A few songs later, he'd found his groove. He was in the zone. The world, and all his frustrations, faded away as the music took over. Wade lost himself to the surround sound and the rhythm of the drumbeats. Closing his eyes, he let his imagination run riot, his body following as he layered the backbeats with complicated licks. His arms and his spirits were flying.

Eventually winding down, Wade opened his eyes to find Eva-Marie standing in his doorway. He froze. Where had she come from, and how long had she been standing there? Slowly, he laid down his sticks, then reached for his remote control, half expecting her to disappear like some sexy mirage. He shut off the music, but before he could get a word out, Eva-Marie was nervously babbling, the same way she'd done in his parents' kitchen.

"I hope you don't mind me coming up here without an invitation. I'm sorry for intruding. The gates were still open, and I rang the bell, but the music was so loud I was sure you couldn't hear it. The door was already open. If it's not a good time I can go." The words tumbled from her so fast he could barely keep up.

"No," Wade interrupted. "It's fine." He stepped away from the drums. Just give me a second to clean up a bit." Grabbing a towel he'd draped across a barstool after his shower, he scrubbed his face and hair, attempting to dry off some of the sweat. Moving the towel down to wipe his neck, he noticed Eva-Marie still standing in the doorway.

"Come on in. Make yourself at home."

Wade rubbed his chest and abs briskly, trying to covertly swab his sweaty armpits. But instead of going to the sofa as he expected, she dropped her purse and keys on the table by the door and walked directly to him. Without a word, she took the towel from him and stretched it out. Moving behind him, she drew the soft, fluffy cotton along his skin. Each slow wipe was a sensual caress. He could feel the warmth of her touch through the terrycloth, tracing electric patterns across his back.

The teasing torture he was already enduring was nothing compared to the agony of her attention when she came around to the front. Her movements slowed to a crawl as she gave his chest and abdomen her full concentration. The softness of her brushes across his nipples, and the drag of her nails against the towel as her fingers roamed through the hair on his chest almost drove him crazy. Every line of his six-pack abs was traced with the utmost care, while her warm breath fanned across his chest.

His skin practically quivered under her touches. His cock stood up and reached for her. Dammit, if Eva-Marie didn't stop, he was going to embarrass himself like a high school virgin. Taking hold of her wrists, he brought his wonderful torment to a halt.

"Em." Her whole name was too much to handle at the moment. He could barely get the harsh whisper of the nickname past the lump in his throat. "You're going to start something I'm not sure I can stop." Wade needed to give her the opportunity to back off before he acted on the pressing need in his heart, and his pants.

Eva-Marie looked up at him, a naughty twinkle in her wide, tawny eyes. She made no effort to free herself from his grasp. Instead, dropping the towel, she blinked innocently up at him, and inched a little closer.

"Sorry," she said, her tone letting him know she wasn't sorry at all. "I was enjoying myself. I didn't mean to make you *uncomfortable*."

So, she was aware of his stiff cock, even though she hadn't looked at it or come in contact with it at all. *The princess wanted to play with fire, eh? Fine.*

Releasing her wrists, he executed a swift move and scooped her into his arms, shocking a tiny shriek from her lips. Stalking over to the big leather sectional sofa cradling his prize, Wade twisted, falling onto his back. He held Eva-Marie close to absorb the impact of the fall, and to take pleasure in the feel of her amazing body against his. Her curves fit into his arms like he was made to hold her. Curly chestnut hair cascaded across his face, and he inhaled the rich, herbal scent of her shampoo. It wasn't the flowery, girly scent he expected from the princess, but damn if it wasn't acting like a magical substitute for a little blue pill.

Wriggling in his arms, Eva-Marie slid around on top of Wade, making herself comfortable. Her hands moved over his shoulders and down his biceps, and she raised her head to speak to him.

"I knew you were strong, but wow." Her already husky voice was slightly deeper, breathless. He flexed automatically when she squeezed his biceps, suppressing a smile at the catch in her breath.

She dropped her head back to his chest, nuzzling her cheek against the mat of curly hair that had grown since he'd been home. No manscaping when he wasn't on tour was his personal policy. When Eva-Marie gave a slight, needy little moan, he knew he'd made the right choice. Bringing a hand to his chest, she smoothed her fingers reverently across the hair on one side, continuing to snuggle her cheek into the other side.

If this was her idea of a seduction, it was the sweetest one he'd ever seen. And it was working like a fucking charm. Wade had never been this turned on in his life, especially since there were still so many clothes between them.

He ran his hands down Eva-Marie's back, and she answered by arching into his caresses, rocking her hips and pressing against his hard length. They moaned in unison. Slipping his hands beneath her tee shirt, Wade stroked the flawless silk of her skin. He hoped like hell she wouldn't find his calloused palms repulsive, but he needed to touch her too badly to stop himself.

Instead of pulling away, she rained kisses across his chest. He watched her tongue dart out and lap at the tiny nub of his nipple when she reached it, shivering at the sensation it caused. Wade groaned deep in his chest and reached down to fill his hands with the fantastic flesh of her denim-covered ass, and rolled his hips so his hardness pressed into her softness.

"Mmm," she murmured against his chest, parting her legs to straddle his, so his cock was cradled against her mound. "You feel good."

"Em, seriously," Wade managed to get out through gritted teeth. "Stop now, or we're not stopping."

She kissed him. A scorching hot, devastating kiss that broke him down to a needy, horny high school kid again. He felt her in every cell in his body, as if she was the lifeblood flowing through his veins. For a split second, she released his mouth, and there was a brush of fabric across his cheek. But when he opened his eyes to see what was happening, all he could see was a curtain of russet curls. Then, her lips were upon his once again, and his mind was overtaken by whatever magic spell she was weaving over him.

While his tongue tangled with hers, his hands

were busy too, roaming her body, memorizing every inch she'd uncovered by shedding her shirt. Her skin, smoother than silk and warmer than cashmere, branded him with fire wherever they touched. Eva-Marie had left her personal mark on him, and Wade was happy to be claimed.

His fingers searched along the strap at her back for the closure to her bra, but there wasn't one. *In the front.* Sliding his hands between their bodies, he cupped her lace-covered breasts in his palms and gently massaged before attempting to free them. *Not a problem.*

Someone moaned. Wade wasn't sure if it was her or him. Eva-Marie trembled in his arms, her nipples pebbling in his palms through a barely-there scrap of lace. He squeezed her sweet mounds of flesh, smooshing them together so he could reach the center clasp without releasing his hold on his prizes. Finally liberating them from their lacy prison, he wiggled his fingers to pinch and roll her taut nipples, priming them for his lips and tongue.

Breaking their kiss at last, he reached down to lift Eva-Marie to his hungry and waiting mouth, enjoying the added pleasure of her body dragging along his. Nibbling his way down her neck to her chest, Wade made it to his promised land, and froze at the sight of her bright red bra.

"Wade?" Eva-Marie looked confused as she stared down at him. "What's wrong? Did I do something you didn't like?"

Setting her away from him as gently as possible, he sat up, dragging his hands across his face. It was just lingerie, he knew, but the effect on him was like a bucket of ice water to the balls. An immediate flash of Eva-Marie, lying halfway underneath Scott went through his mind. His hands were on her skin, and that damned red bra she was wearing that night, the one that changed his whole life, shone like neon.

"Shit." Rising, he stalked to the refrigerator and grabbed a beer. He offered her one, but she shook her head and continued pulling her bra back into place and refastening the clasp. He frowned, watching her every move.

"Your problem with me, tell me what it is." Eva-Marie relaxed against the pillows on the sofa, folding her arms and glaring at him.

"You're going to think I'm crazy."

She remained stock still and deathly quiet, her face completely unreadable.

Wade sighed heavily.

"Your bra."

"What about it?" The words were clipped like she was angry, her accent slightly more noticeable.

Taking a long swig from the beer bottle, Wade gathered the nerve to tell her what she wanted to know. He cleared his throat and spoke, rushing through the explanation to get it over with as fast as he could.

"It's red. Like the night I saw you making out with Scott. The night I got wasted and ended up in jail."

Eva-Marie bolted up, eyes wide as silver dollars, mouth hanging open in shock. Her hand rose up, seemingly of its own accord, and covered her gaping mouth. She stared at him for what felt like forever before she said anything.

"You saw us?"

"Not everything." He grimaced, replaying the memory in his head for the two millionth time. "Just enough to see where things were headed between you and my brother." Wade chugged the rest of his beer and set the bottle aside, then jammed his hands in his pockets to keep from fidgeting during the most uncomfortable fucking conversation of his life.

"It makes me wonder," he continued, "and not for the first time, why you're here with me now. Why the sudden interest in me?"

Her frown brought a fierceness to her face he'd never seen before.

"Why do you think?"

Wade knew his answer could determine whether anything ever happened between them. All he could do was tell her the truth, and hope for the best, whatever the hell that was.

"Honestly, I think I might be a substitute for Scott, since you guys aren't intimate any more. I don't want it to be true, but the thought has crossed my mind."

"I see."

Eva-Marie reached down and retrieved her shirt from the floor, where she'd carelessly tossed it earlier in the midst of their passion. She pulled it over her head and settled it on her body, then lifted her hair from the collar, shaking her curls into place. Each move seemed slow and careful, as if she was deliberately mocking him with her seductive beauty. Every gesture said *if you weren't acting silly, you could be touching this right now.*

"You should have stayed to watch the rest of it." Her voice was flat, her eyes challenging him to believe her explanation. "You would have seen that nothing happened."

"Nothing?"

"Not a thing. Neither of our hearts was in it. When we talked, we discovered that each of us had a thing for someone else. Scott and I care for each other very much, but only as friends."

Wade was stunned. All these years he'd thought Scott had a claim on Eva-Marie's heart, and he was wrong. Dead wrong. Shock wasn't a strong enough word for what he was feeling.

She stood watching him process the new information, a look of profound sadness now on her pretty face. Fuck. He'd taken the light right out of her eyes. Right now, he felt like the biggest prick on the planet. No doubt, she would agree.

"You know, Wade," she began, sounding thoughtful and eerily calm, "it occurs to me that your interest is somewhat sudden as well. You've barely ever looked at me before I asked you out. Now you're ready for seduction at the slightest touch. What gives? Am I just another groupie to you? Or perhaps I'm the one who's a substitute for someone else?"

He had not been expecting that from Eva-Marie, and didn't know what to say. Not that it mattered, because she wasn't listening anyway. Before he realized her intention, she was at the door, snatching up her things and moving through it quicker than a ghost, closing it quietly behind her. If she had slammed it, he could have held on to the hope that maybe they could talk after she calmed down. But the quiet click of his door shutting was as final as any goodbye he'd ever heard.

CHAPTER
5

All morning, Wade was distracted and forgetful. A couple of times, his mind went blank when he answered the phone. Only Chad and BJ yelling "Boost Turtle" in the background prompted him to recite their standard business greeting. They laughed their asses off when he reddened with embarrassment.

Opting to leave the phones to Chad, Wade decided to work on one of the project cars instead. Keeping his hands busy under a hood was great when he had some heavy thinking to do. Today, however, even that was a bust. After spending an hour installing, removing, and reinstalling one part, only to realize he hadn't done the custom modifications yet, he'd had all he could stand. Especially of his friends high fiving and calling out "Boost Turtle" every time he did something stupid, which was a lot. He was sick to death of those two words, at least for one day.

Wiping his hands and tossing the shop towels aside, Wade headed upstairs to shower, so he could do what he'd really wanted to all day long—find Eva-Marie and apologize. The more time passed, the more he felt like a total heel. If he got a move on, he might be in time to beg her to have lunch with him. The special of the day was humble pie.

Phoning her office from the car, he learned she'd taken the day off. Wade hoped she was okay. Maybe, like him, she just wasn't in the right frame of mind to get much done. Her house and cell phones both sent him directly to voicemail.

Now, he was worried. If she didn't want to talk, that was fine. As long as everything else was all right.

Driving to her house, Wade was relieved to see her car there. His relief was short-lived. Her door was answered by the housekeeper, who informed him that Ms. Robinson was unavailable. When pressed, she let him know that Eva-Marie was out of town, but only then because she recognized his name as one of the people who had access to her at home. It was a good sign that she hadn't kicked him off her friends list. Yet. He thanked the lady and walked back to his car.

She was gone. Some time in the hours since last night and lunchtime today, Eva-Marie had taken off. Was she that pissed at him, or was something else going on? He brooded about it all the way back to the shop, where he went upstairs and made a sandwich that he barely touched. A soda grew warm in the glass while Wade stared off into space. Did she hate him now? He could practically see the smoke coming from her heels when she left him last night. She couldn't get away from him fast enough, and he couldn't really blame her. He'd sounded like a jealous teenager, going on about his brother and her bra, while she was in the middle of making love to him. He was a fucking idiot, and it showed.

Instead of just telling her how much he'd cared for her all along, he'd let Eva-Marie walk away from him feeling like a groupie. She was a princess, but he was no prince for sure. He should never have let her feel that way for a single second. If she never spoke to him again, he deserved that, and more.

If he was lucky, she'd give him the chance to beg her forgiveness and explain what a fool he was, wasting all that time obsessing about something that never happened. The whole time, he'd thought her heart belonged to Scott. Twice, she'd told him they were friends, and he'd maintained his assumptions instead of listening to her. Was he so blinded by his own jealousy, he couldn't see the truth right in front of his own eyes?

Yeah, he'd fucked up royally. And Eva-Marie was nowhere to be found, so he couldn't apologize. It was driving him mad. Taking a chance, he dialed her cellphone again, groaning when it went to voicemail. Defeated, Wade got up to clean his lunch mess and go back down to work. There was nothing he could do until she wanted to be bothered with him, if she ever did. Right now, he almost missed being on tour. At least then, he was too busy to think much. But who was he kidding? No matter what, practically every thought was still of Eva-Marie.

****

Wade flopped down on the sofa with a beer in one hand and his phone in the other. Hard to believe that just twenty-four hours ago, Eva-Marie was with him on this very spot, kissing him and ready for more. *Damn, he was an idiot.* He couldn't kick himself enough. Who flaked out when the woman of his dreams was in his arms? That shit was only supposed to happen on the movie of the week.

Taking a deep pull on the beer for courage, he dialed Eva-Marie once again. Her phone rang twice, then he heard a mumbled, "'Lo?"

Shocked speechless, he sat straight up, mouth opened in surprise, almost dropping the bottle.

There were fumbling noises in his ear, then she spoke again.

"Hello? Wade?"

"Uh, hi. Hi, Eva-Marie," he finally managed to stammer. "I wasn't really expecting you to answer. Caught me off guard. I called earlier, a couple of times."

"Oh, well my cell has been off for most of the day. I've been in non-stop meetings until just a little while ago. I turned it on about fifteen minutes ago and saw a lot of missed calls and messages, but I'm too tired to deal with any of it tonight. I didn't even look at them. Sorry. Was it something important? Is everyone okay?"

Wade was already unsure of how to approach the subject of their encounter the night before. The situation was too awkward. Now it seemed she'd shut herself off from him emotionally.

There was no warmth in her voice at all. No matter how much he deserved that from her, actually getting it was still more painful than he'd imagined.

"Everyone is fine. I was calling to apologize for my behavior last night. The things I said, and how I made you feel. I never, ever meant to do that. I know you probably won't believe it, but you've always been special to me. I should have told you that."

There was silence on the line for too long.

"Eva-Marie?"

"I'm here."

"If you're busy, we can talk some other time."

"I'm in my pyjamas eating a salad," she answered, giving a short, harsh laugh. "I've had a long day, and after last night, I haven't been in the greatest mood. So, just give me a moment to process everything, okay?"

"Whatever you want," Wade agreed quickly.

"You know, Wade, Scott let people think we were dating when we were younger. We both did. It took care of a lot of social situations that could have been really messy for Scott or me if we hadn't been part of a couple. Being *with each other* saved us, in a way. I know that sounds silly."

"Nah, I get it," Wade assured her. "I remember Scott's girl trouble before you moved here. All the ridiculous things they would do to get close to him or spend time around him. It was crazy, even scary sometimes. Still is. All the girls want to be with the rock star. I imagine all the boys were the same way about the ambassador's daughter from Down Under."

"I remember you getting some of that, too. And I'm sure it's still going on, Mr. Bad Boy Rock Star," Eva-Marie countered.

"A little," he conceded, "but nothing like it is for him. Besides," he said with a laugh, "I think my fans are afraid of me. I'm always frowning at them."

"Yeah, I know what that's like. But it got way out of hand for Scott and me," Eva-Marie continued. "I mean, I expected a bit of interest. I'm sort of a foreigner, since I mostly grew up in Australia. And I've gotten to meet presidents and royalty because of my father's job. Then someone decided I was secretly a princess one day, and all hell broke loose. It got to the point my dad threatened to remove me from the school, which I was really starting to love. Or he was sending in a bodyguard. You can imagine how much worse that would have been. I would have just died."

Wade chuckled at her teen speak, but he understood what she meant. A bodyguard would have basically confirmed the rumor in people's minds, and the result would have been chaos.

"Then Scott got the idea to be my fake boyfriend. He said I'd be doing him a favor, but it was the best solution for both of us. It worked, and eventually everything calmed down. But I had no idea you witnessed our little experiment with dating each other. I don't blame you for thinking what you did. I do, however, blame you for not coming to me and talking about your concerns."

"You're right, I should have, especially if it was bothering me. I feel so silly now that I know nothing happened. I'm so sorry."

Eva-Marie took a deep breath.

"There's something else."

Uh-oh. No good conversation starts this way.

"After the last twenty-four hours, I'm not sure I can take any bad news." Wade attempted to both lighten the mood and put himself at her mercy. *Please don't decide to end things before they get started.*

"You were right about my interest in you seeming sudden and out-of-character. I've always been rather reserved around you, mostly because I believed you didn't like me much. Now I'm coming to your house and your job, practically throwing myself at you. It does look a bit suspicious. After the way things turned out, I'm thinking I should just call this a fail and go back to the way things were."

No. Wade couldn't lose her, not when he was so close to his dream come true. Not to mention, having her doubt the inner seductress she was finally setting free.

"If I may, I'd like to weigh in on that." It was

possibly his last chance to turn things around between them. "I think it's completely incorrect to label this a fail. It was going pretty well until I messed things up."

"Yeah, right." She snorted, sounding disgusted. "My big seduction turned into a big fight. And unless I'm mistaken, you were *not* interested in being seduced."

"I was extremely interested," Wade insisted. "There was, uh, outside interference."

Eva-Marie burst into laughter. Making her laugh was promising, he hoped. Maybe a second chance wasn't off the table for good.

"While we're on that subject, when you get home, why don't you throw away all your red bras."

"I am home. And do you know how much a good bra costs? Have you lost your mind?"

Wait, what did she say?

"You're in Memphis, Eva-Marie?" Wade jumped up, searching around for his jeans and shoes. "I could come over there. We could get everything settled tonight."

"No." She immediately shut him down. "It's late, and I'm tired. Besides, I'm not ready to see you again yet. I'm still a little shell shocked from yesterday. That sort of thing doesn't happen to a woman every day. Besides, the groupie thing. It's a valid point. You need to think about it, Wade. Other than sleeping with me, what do you want?"

She said a quick goodnight, and other than some muttering about how good she looked in red, it was the last thing he heard before the line went dead. Eva-Marie was gone, and he wasn't sure she was coming back to him.

CHAPTER
6

For two days, radio silence. Wade forced himself not to call Eva-Marie, or give in to his incessant desire to see her. He was trying to respect her wishes and give her the space she needed, but it was killing him to do so. Their conversation played over and over in his mind, bothering him more each time. As happy as he was to find out nothing happened between her and Scott, her comment about still feeling like a groupie sliced him straight to the heart. He'd apologized, but it wasn't enough. Regret over the hurt he'd caused her made him almost physically ill.

Much of his time over the last forty-eight hours had been spent under the hood of his car, deep in thought, wondering how he could make amends with Eva-Marie. He wanted her to understand exactly how special she was to him. He would explain until he was blue in the face, then show her until he was too weak to move. Then do it all again, as many times as necessary until she believed he meant every word. It wasn't simply wanting sex, like she thought. It was letting her know she'd been the only one for him since she was sixteen years old. She was the object of his lust, true. But also of his fantasies, and definitely of his love. His puppy love, high school crush had matured over time into the real thing.

This was not the time to speak to Eva-Marie of love, though. Considering they'd done most of their talking so far with their hands and hormones, she probably wouldn't trust a word he said anyway. She was so sure he only wanted to fuck her. Made him sound like a real dick, no pun intended. She knew him better than that, and if she didn't, she should. Shouldn't she?

Frowning, his hands came to a standstill where they'd been polishing the last of the dirt and oily fingerprints from the car. Thinking about it from her perspective, maybe not. From where she stood, his interest did appear to be suspiciously quick. In addition, he hadn't exactly jumped at the chance to go out with her.

Distracted by the sound of a car driving up to the garage, Wade stood to see who was coming by after closing time. A few seconds later, Scott strolled in, looking every inch the rock star, even though they hadn't been on stage in weeks. His grin was huge.

"What the hell do you want, you long-haired freak?" Wade was always happy to see his brother.

Scott came over to him and slung his arm across Wade's shoulders.

"I heard there was a dusty grease monkey

around here. I came to see for myself." Wade was pulled into Scott's embrace, which resembled a headlock more than a hug, with Scott's hearty laughter ringing in his ears.

"Just coming by to see how things are going with you." Disentangling himself, Scott grabbed one of the rolling stools and plopped down on it.

"I'm good," Wade responded, leaning against the car. "But you're going to ruin your designer duds down here in all this dirt. You want to go up to the house?"

"Nah." Scott used the stool to spin around a few times, then zoomed back and forth down the narrow passage between the cars before coming to a stop by his brother. He was giggling like an overgrown child.

Watching him, Wade chuckled and shook his head. Scott was crazy. So quiet and well-behaved, until people really got to know him. Then he was a total clown. He was still spinning on that stool like a nut. This was the rock star, idolized by millions. Hysterical.

"So, what's up with you and my girl?" Scott

asked casually. "I know you and Eva-Marie are seeing each other. Come on, spill. You know I'm curious."

Crossing his arms defensively, Wade glared at Scott as he pushed the stool from side to side with his feet. He had some nerve asking for details about the two of them. They'd never shared intimate details about women before, and considering Scott's past with Eva-Marie, he felt weird about being asked.

Gazing off into space, Scott kept talking. "She was always so damn sexy. Still is. Did I tell you I kissed her once?"

Wade was instantly on his feet, wild eyed, fists clenched. He hovered over Scott, wanting more than anything to deck him right then. Though they'd barely fought as children, and never as adults, the comment about Eva-Marie went to far as far as he was concerned.

"Dude," he growled menacingly, "don't make me fuck up that pretty face of yours."

Scott stared at him, looking startled, and more than a little scared. He quickly rolled the stool out of Wade's reach.

"Hey, man, what's your damned problem?"

"Don't ever speak about her like that again, or I promise you I'll break your fucking jaw. Understand?" Wade glowered at Scott, making it clear he meant every word.

Scott was quiet, a tiny smirk eventually appearing on his face.

"Yeah, I understand, bro. Better thank you think."

Wade watched his brother spin on his seat again, dragging his hand through his hair. It was his telltale signal that he was upset or irritated. When their eyes met again, he thought Scott looked a little run down. As his fury dissipated, he wondered what was on Scott's mind. Was something bothering him? Taking a chance, he tried to find out.

"Out with it," he told his little brother.

"You know Eva-Marie was never actually my girlfriend, right? In fact, back in high school, my mind was on someone else. The only girl I've never been able to get out of my head. She was something else- the smartest person I'd ever met, pretty, and sweet." Scott looked almost forlorn talking about this girl, whoever she was.

"I was shitty to her, Wade. A real asshole. I felt bad about it then, and even worse now."

Wade crossed his arms again and frowned at his younger brother. Scott had never been a mean kid. Not to anyone. He'd been shy and standoffish, so there must have been a reason for his rough treatment of the girl. Whatever it was, it was eating at him now. Poor guy. He felt bad for him.

"What are you going to do about it?"

"Try to apologize to her, if she'll let me." Scott sighed heavily.

"Good luck with that." Wade meant it, knowing exactly how it felt to be in that position.

"Anyway," Scott continued, "back to Eva-Marie. She's an amazing girl. Well, woman. But I always suspected she had a thing for you, even back in school."

Wade couldn't believe what he was hearing. Apparently unaware of his shock, Scott kept rambling on.

"She's always asking about you. I give her hell for it all the time. I love her, man, but it's more like I'd love a sister, if you get my drift."

Stunned, Wade tried to remember if Eva-Marie had ever given any indication before now that she was into him, and came up blank. But, she'd asked him out first. And there was no question she wanted him. If she'd been waiting as long as he had, it was no wonder she'd moved a little fast. He'd wanted like hell to do the same. Only his uncertainty about her feelings and motives held him back. Now Scott was telling him she'd always been interested in him. After all this time, they'd finally decided to let him in on their secret.

"Why make a move now, then?" Wade pinned Scott with a stare that dared him to waffle about the answer or joke his way out of it. "If she's always liked me, why wait until now to let me know?"

"For the longest time, she thought you couldn't stand her. You were always scowling at her when she was at our house. Or you would grunt when she spoke to you, and act like you couldn't wait to get away from her. I've tried to talk her into flirting with you for years. I told her you'd go for her in a big way. Me and my big mouth. I practically shoved her in the kitchen and made her face you, finally, and you acted all crazy and insulted her."

Wade blushed at the memory of that night.

"Yeah, I heard about it." Scott kept talking, on a roll. "She hasn't said anything since then, so I wanted to make sure you were being nice to her. She's still my closest friend." This time Scott was the one looking fierce.

"We're fine. She's a little miffed at me, but I'm going to handle that as soon as I'm done here."

"Good deal. I love you, dude, but we're going to have a problem if you hurt my best girl."

"No worries, man," Wade reassured Scott. "That's not in the plans."

"All right then." Scott rose from his perch on the stool. "I'll go be amazing elsewhere."

Wade rolled his eyes at his crazy sibling, who responded with exaggerated primping and striking a pose like a runway model.

"Boost Turtle," Scott growled in a ridiculous, pseudo-sexy accent.

"Get the fuck out." Wade gave him a playful push when they could finally stop laughing.

"Later, man," Scott responded with a wave, making his way back to his car.

Hurriedly cleaning the rest of the car, Wade rushed upstairs to get cleaned up. He took a little extra care with his appearance. If he was going to drag Eva-Marie out of bed and convince her to hear him out, a little cologne and hair gel couldn't hurt. His intention was to go to her house, bang on her door, and plead his case once she let him in. When he arrived, the big house was so dark and imposing, he chickened out.

Picking up his phone, he tapped the screen and dialed her number. Though the device was pressed to his ear, he couldn't hear a thing over his own pounding heartbeat. Switching to the speaker, he finally heard it ring. Once more, and she answered.

"Wade?"

"Hey. Did I wake you?"

"No," she told him. "I'm up."

"Can we talk now, or is it a bad time?" Silently praying that his impulsiveness would be rewarded, he waited for her response.

"Now is fine. We can talk."

Wade released the breath he was holding, slumping in relief.

"Good. I've missed you, Eva-Marie. Come let me in, honey. I need to see you. Please?"

"You're here?" She sounded understandably shocked.

"I'm right outside."

The phone went dead.

Barely a minute later, the front door swung open. Wade met her at the door and pulled her into his arms, taking a moment to just enjoy holding Eva-Marie again before following her into the house.

CHAPTER
7

Eva-Marie still held Wade's hand as she led him down the hallway into her comfortable study. He was finally with her again. It felt like much longer than two days since she'd seen him. Now that they were together again, there was one thing she was determined to take care of. Whatever lingering doubts he had about Scott, they were going to settle them tonight.

As soon as Eva-Marie switched on the light, Wade dragged her to the nearest sofa and pulled her down beside him. He wrapped her in his strong arms once more, like he needed to hold her. She snuggled into his embrace because it felt so good to be held.

"I really, really missed you."

She heard the words Wade murmured against her skin as he nuzzled her neck above the fuzzy, cream colored robe.

"Good," she said sweetly, "it wouldn't do for me to be the only one."

She felt his deep chuckle rumble through his body first, then through hers. Involuntarily, she shivered, and Wade's hold on her tightened. He pressed a kiss to Eva-Marie's cheek, surprising her.

"I wasn't going to make it much longer without seeing you," Wade confessed. "It was driving me crazy. All I could think about was you."

"What were you thinking?" Eva-Marie drew away from Wade until she could look him in the eyes. His answer mattered. After waiting so long to truly get to know Wade, she was interested in what he thought, especially about her.

"That you should probably know I've been into you since high school. Like everyone else, I thought you were Scott's girlfriend, so I never said anything."

"You're kidding." Eva-Marie couldn't believe her ears.

"It's true. I was as fascinated by you as every other boy. You were beautiful and exotic and brilliant. You still are."

"Wow. Thank you." She was blushing under his praise. "I never would have guessed."

"I didn't want to be disrespectful to my brother, or make things complicated for you guys. But now that we've gotten all that cleared up, we can forget about it and move on."

"Okay," she agreed, glad to be done with that subject.

"Wait." Wade took one of Eva-Marie's hands in his and brought it to his lips, sending a little frisson of tingly heat spreading up her arm and throughout her body. His expression was serious as he gazed at her intensely. Whatever was

86

coming next, he appeared to feel strongly about it.

"I need to say something else before this... before we go any farther. You have to know this isn't casual for me. It's my fault for not making that clear before. This thing between us, it's about more than sex for me. In fact, we can wait on that, if you want. Do you think that would be better?" He squeezed her hand. "Anything you wish is okay by me, honey."

Eva-Marie looked deeply into the dark, earnest eyes of the man she'd wanted for what felt like her whole life.

"That's nice to know. I'm glad you feel that way, because I don't want this to be a casual fling either, Wade. I'd like for us to have something real, or to at least try. And no, I don't want to wait. I think we've both waited long enough. Don't you?"

She rose, pulling him up from the sofa by the hand he still held. Then, beckoning for Wade to follow her, Eva-Marie led the way up the stairs to her bedroom. The thick carpet masked the sounds of their footsteps, and she wondered if Wade could hear the rapid thumping of her heart in the quiet house. Earlier that evening, she'd already decided not to miss out on what could be her one chance to be with the one man she'd always loved. She was planning to call him tomorrow and tell him so, but he'd beat her to the draw, thank goodness. Knowing he missed her was amazing, as was the fact he wanted a real relationship, not just one night. From the moment he'd said those words, she'd been more relaxed and confident. And even more ready to make love to him.

In her room, Eva-Marie dropped the robe and stood before Wade in a short, purple stretch lace nightie. She wore no bra underneath, she he had a peekaboo glimpse of her breasts through the lace. The tiniest of straps held up the gown, which only hung down a couple of inches past her hips and ass. Her purple string bikini panties matched the nightie, and probably showed as much as they covered.

Wade cleared his throat.

"Do you always sleep dressed like that?" His voice was low and husky, and his gaze roamed over her as if he was trying to memorize everything he saw.

"Yes, I always wear nice lingerie. It helps keep me in a good mood. You know, a woman looks pretty when she feels pretty. Or, something like that." Her voice faded, and she blushed. The way Wade was looking at her was making her a little breathless. Already having a dark and dangerous appearance, right now he looked positively savage.

Wade moved toward Eva-Marie, and for every step he took, she backed up one, suddenly nervous in the face of this wild man she'd invited to her bedroom. Wade was stalking her like he was a hungry predator, and she was destined to be his feast.

"Em," he sighed. Wade's breaths came heavily and fast, and hers matched them, her chest heaving in time with his.

When he finally slid his arm around her waist and pulled her body against his, Eva-Marie almost moaned out loud with relief. She wanted Wade so very much. The press of his shaft against her belly let her know he was probably feeling the same way. There had better not be any interruptions this time. She was certain she wouldn't be able to take another night like the first one.

Wade brushed a curl away from her face, his touch gentle despite the fierce look in his eyes.

"Em, baby?"

She shivered in his arms as his husky whisper traveled over her skin like a feather-light touch.

"Yes." At the moment, it was the answer to everything.

"The first time's going to be hard and fast. I don't think I'll be able to help it. After that, we can make love. Any way you want. As many times as you want. I promise. Okay, honey?"

Eva-Marie stared into Wade's gorgeous dark eyes. Hard. Fast. Perfect.

"Yes. Now." She reached for his mouth.

****

The second her lips met his, Wade lost control. Eva-Marie was in his arms again, and he was going to make love with her. Tonight. Nothing was going to stop him- no ghosts from the past, and no disruptions in the present.

He kissed her with all the passion he'd felt for her since the day they'd met. In his arms, she melted, draping herself around his body, and slithering sensuously against him, teasing his cock into a degree of hardness he'd never known before. And still he kissed her, coaxing her open and ravaging every iota of space inside her mouth while his hands roamed her lace-covered body.

When Wade could tear himself away from the delicious temptation of Eva-Marie's lips, he eased her away from him. Gently, he lifted the straps of the nightgown away from her skin, and let them fall. He followed the descent of the lace extremely closely, marveling over every beautiful inch of skin as it was revealed.

"God, you're magnificent."

The awe he felt was evident in his voice, in

the way he couldn't take his eyes off her, and in the swift way he was back at her side, as if he couldn't wait to touch her again. Wade undressed in a blur of motion that could have made a racecar driver dizzy. Pulling Eva-Marie back into his arms, he moved to the bed and sat down, pulling her with him to straddle his lap.

When she instinctively grabbed his shoulders to hold on, Wade leaned in to trail kisses across her chest and throat, his excitement amplified by the appearance of goosebumps in the wake of his lips as they moved along her skin. Going lower, he nuzzled at her breast.

"Em." Her name was a long, low moan before he softly rolled her nipple between his teeth, then sucked it into his mouth. Hearing Eva-Marie draw in a hissing breath Wade looked up to see her eyes drifting closed. Her head fell back as she arched and pressed her breast closer to his suckling lips. He felt her caressing his shoulders, stroking her fingers along the plains of his jawline, then plunging her hands into his hair, gripping the short waves and holding his head to her breast.

Sliding his hands down her back, Wade slipped them into the purple panties. He filled his hands with the bounty of her of her sublimely plump, round ass. Squeezing and massaging her supple flesh, he pressed upward with his hips while pulling her down onto the hard ridge of his cock. Reluctantly dragging his mouth away from her breast, he groaned in frustration.

"Fuck, Em, I can't wait."

"Don't."

She'd barely gotten the word out when Wade lifted her, moving the panties to the side, and impaling her on his cock. They both cried out in unison.

"Ah," Wade groaned. "Damn, sweetheart. You're so fucking tight."

"Oh." Eva-Marie squeezed her thighs alongside his and her hands dropped to his shoulders again. Wade felt her nails digging into his skin, making him pause momentarily.

Releasing his grip on his darling's gorgeous ass, Wade dragged his fingers slowly down her thighs to her knees. Drawing soothing circles there, he attempted to get her to relax.

"Em," he crooned, resting his forehead against hers. "Look at me, baby."

He continued to stroke her thighs, listening to her panting softly as he waited for her to adjust to him. She'd said she was ready, but he was possibly too forceful in his haste. And she was so, so tight. He could feel every fluctuation of the muscles inside her, gripping his shaft in time with her rhythmic breathing. Every millimeter he sank deeper inside her was torture. Sweet and wonderful, but torture all the same.

He felt like the world's biggest jackass for rushing, and for hurting her when she was only trying to please him. It was the last thing he wanted to do. How the hell was he supposed to apologize for this one?

Her eyes were still squeezed shut, but she'd eased the death grip with her thighs a bit. Her nails penetrated slightly less deeply into his shoulders and back.

"Come on, love," he encouraged her, "open

94

your eyes."

Eva-Marie's eyelids fluttered open seemingly against her will.

"That's it, baby."

She blinked like she was waking up from a trance. Her normally golden-brown eyes had darkened to cinnamon colored pools of liquid heat. And the way she was looking at Wade was likely to set him on fire. Holy fuck.

"Wade." It was somewhere between a whisper and a sigh. Her breath fanned across his lips as sweetly as a kiss.

"Em, honey, talk to me." He pulled away, cupping her chin to make sure he had her attention. "Did I hurt you, baby? Are you okay?"

She quirked her lips in a little smile and closed her eyes again, her head falling back as he watched in confusion.

"Mmm," Eva-Marie moaned, her hips moving, twitching the tiniest bit.

Wade drew in a sharp breath between his teeth. His cock throbbed inside her. He couldn't help it. She jumped slightly in response, shifted a little, then oh, so slowly circled her ass, pushing him deeper into her hot, slick sheath.

Judging by her answer, she was fine. He would still take it slow, since he could tell she was still having trouble accommodating him. But every rotation of her pussy on his cock was magic. Exactly as he'd somehow known it would be.

A few more sexy twirls of her hips, and his enchanting princess had him fully seated inside her. A groan of pleasure so strong he couldn't suppress it bubbled up into his chest, clutching his heart, before emerging as her name. She hugged him closer, and he wrapped his arms around her, savoring their connection.

Running his calloused hands down the delicate softness of her back, he thrilled when she shivered under his touch. His princess. He rocked into her, and she buried her face in his neck and purred.

"Mmm." Her lips were pressed against his throat, and the vibrations from her moan shot straight down to his cock.

"Good," Eva-Marie whispered between kisses and bites on his skin. "So good."

"Damn it, woman." Wade growled his passion and frustration. "You're going to make me cum in two minutes like a teenager."

He felt, more than heard, her chuckle. *So, she thinks this is funny, huh. Let's see if she thinks this is funny as well.* Cupping her ass, he held her to his body while he pistoned his hips and drove into her wet, amazing heat.

"Ohhh."

Not exactly laughter from the princess. She'd raised her knees and planted her feet on the bed, then linked her hands behind his neck. Now she was bucking in his arms like a cowgirl, bouncing on him as hard as he was driving into her.

Shit. He'd pushed a button and turned on her inner porn star. And sweet princess Eva-Marie was going to fuck his brains out. He was barely holding on to his sanity, trying to hang on to her beautiful body.

"Baby," he huffed through clenched teeth. "Gotta... slow... down. Gonna cum." Wade finally had his dream girl, and she was going to break him.

"No." Her whisper was husky and demanding. "Now."

Wade didn't want to give in, but he didn't have much choice. If he lasted more than another minute, it would be a miracle.

"Em." Her name was a heartfelt plea. "Sweetheart, we have to slow- I'm trying- ."

"Now, Wade!"

His name started on a moan and ended on a scream as Eva-Marie came apart in his arms and took him with her.

CHAPTER
8

Every chance he had since that night, Wade made love to Eva-Marie. For hours, sometime days at a stretch. Every evening after work, the would rush to each other for a frantic coupling, then spend the rest of the night in sensual exploration of each other. He couldn't get enough of her, and apparently the feeling was mutual.

But not tonight. Here they were, standing in a club packed with people. Most of the owners of the Beale Street establishments had come by to say hello, along with what seemed to be a million members of the press, one of whom had a microphone shoved belligerently in his face. There were always a few who took his silent scowls as a challenge and insisted on trying to cajole or bully a response from him. It didn't usually work in their favor, but having Eva-Marie near had softened him. He had managed not to growl at anyone all day, and the media types were taking it as encouragement. A few continued to hang around, but this particular one was downright rude. Baring his teeth at the woman with the microphone, tonight's version of a smile, Wade turned away and stepped directly into the last person he expected or wanted to see.

"Wade Davies." Jeremy Fargas clapped him on the shoulder. "Good to see ya, man."

"And you are?" The reporter zipped around him to seize this new opportunity. Her camera guy was hot on her heels.

"F-A-R-G-A-S." Jeremy smiled broadly into

CHANDRA CRAWFORD

the camera. It was no surprise to Wade that Mike Johnson and Steve Handler were with him. They'd been decent on their own, but they both had a tendency to let Jeremy do their thinking for them. When the bullshit that stole a year and a half of his life went down, they, of course, stood by the Fargas assholes and watched without a word. It could have fucked up his entire future if not for the Hunsakers and his brother, who had his back when no one else did. Did they care? Hell no. He doubted if any of them would have ever thought of him again, if they hadn't seen him on t.v.

"I'm an old friend from high school. I grew up with Wade. We all did. Used to hang out together. Just came down to say hey. *Talk about old times.*"

The slight emphasis on the last statement and the subtle squeeze on his shoulder made it clear what Jeremy was hinting at. On the surface, the shit-eating grin he wore never faltered. Mike and Steve just stood mutely behind him.

Already bristling at the rudeness of the

reporter, Wade let his old enemy's implication get to him, and push his last button. He rounded on his former friend, flinging away the offending hand on his body and sneering nastily at the other man.

"Too famous for your old friends now, Wade?" Fargas kept needling him, cocky 'til the end.

"Hah." Wade rolled his eyes and made a disgusted gagging noise. "Yeah, blame it on the fame. I've been at the shop. All my friends have dropped by. I haven't seen you guys, though. You've been avoiding me like I'm a leper, practically since high school. But you couldn't wait to talk to the cameras today. Well, here they are. Ms. Hill, here, will be glad to give you an interview. Just don't lie and say we're friends after what you guys did to me."

From behind him, Wade heard the dull clink of beer bottles knocking together.

"Boost Turtle!" The voices of BJ and Chad rang out as they stepped up beside him, forcing the other men aside.

Jeremy, whose smile had already begun to falter, took one look at BJ and his mouth went completely slack. Wade chuckled, then stepped up close to Jeremy so that only he could hear what Wade was saying.

"Yeah, he's big, isn't he? One punch, and that's your ass. And this one," he tipped his head at Chad, "he's faster than most of the men in the NFL. Just as strong, too. So, if your MO is still sneaking around, doing dirty shit, and calling your daddy, think twice before you try anything. These aren't even the bodyguards. They're just my friends. The real ones."

Turning back to Ms. Hill, Wade tossed off a quick, "Nice to see you again," before greeting Chad and BJ and steering them away.

"Em." Wade finally located Eva-Marie at the front of the club near the door. She wasn't there when he'd looked before, and he frowned, wondering where she'd been. As he watched, she declined an offer of a drink, and eyed the door as if contemplating her escape. In a few steps, he was beside her, enveloping her in his arms.

"Eva-Marie, you remember BJ and Chad, of course." He cuddled her from behind after she exchanged hellos with the guys, and leaned down to nuzzle her curls.

"Why did you disappear?" he whispered to her.

"Five minutes, Mr. Davies," a voice called, and a camera flashed.

"It was a hot, crazy, madhouse back there. Between your friends, your fans, and the press, I felt like I was getting in the way." She gave a nervous laugh. "No embassy event was ever like this."

"Hey, you've been backstage before."

"Yes. Sitting out of the way on a sofa, watching Scott being charming and handling everyone. And you scowling from a corner."

"Well, things are different now. You're my woman." Wade turned Eva-Marie to face him and growled at her when she giggled at his words.

"Your woman?"

"Damn straight. And I want you right beside

104

me. You're never in the way. Got it?" Pushing back a wayward curl, Wade kissed Eva-Marie, not caring who was watching or what would be said about it. When he released her, she blinked up at him with her heavy-lidded dark gold eyes, and his insides melted.

"One minute."

The voice broke through the spell of Eva-Marie's gaze. He placed another quick kiss on her forehead.

"I'll be back to you in a sec. Let the guys or the guards know if you need anything." Wade squeezed her tightly, then pushed through the crowd to get outside to the stage.

****

The band was starting their third song when a woman slid onto the stool next to Eva-Marie. It was obvious the drink she slammed on the table wasn't her first. She adjusted her breasts where they were straining to break free from the top of her dress, then picked up her glass and downed the rest of the contents in one gulp. Then she turned to glare at Eva-Marie.

"I can't remember your name, but I remember you from back in high school. You were always hanging around Scott when I was with Wade. Looks like you're switching it up now."

What the hell? Come to think of it, this woman did look familiar. Back then, there were always a few hungry-looking girls following Wade and his friends around. If anything, this one still had the same air about her. She wore it like perfume. Her name wouldn't come to mind, though.

"From what I remember, Wade was always a free agent. He was never *with* anyone, except maybe in the biblical sense. And I'm sure I'd know, since I've been around the whole time. I've joined them on tour, also. Though, why it would matter to you is beyond me... um. I'm sorry, I've forgotten your name as well."

"Michelle." She huffed, as if irritated by Eva-Marie not knowing her name. "And anyone who's getting with my son's father matters to me. He doesn't need to be around every two-week fling his dad decides to have."

"*Excuse me?*" Eva-Marie was indignant. Neither Scott nor Wade had ever mentioned anything about a child in the family. And Wade would have told her if he had a son. She was sure of it. Fairly sure, anyway.

Michelle pulled her wallet from her purse and slapped a school photo on the table, which she slid over to Eva-Marie with a self-satisfied looking smirk.

"As you can see, he looks just like his father."

The woman across from her faded away with the rest of the world as Eva-Marie stared down at the picture of the scowling boy. His dark brows were drawn together over equally dark eyes. A mop of shaggy black hair stuck out at odd angles over his head, like someone had attempted to give him a hipster haircut and failed miserably. His pale skin, the one feature he might have inherited from the blonde mother, was speckled with the first signs of teenage acne.

The boy could easily be Wade's child. The shape of his face was similar. The slant of his

107

eyebrows, the length of his nose, the same dark eyes and hair. He didn't exactly look like Wade, but he favored him enough to raise some questions.

"This picture doesn't prove anything." Eva-Marie kept her expression carefully neutral.

"Yeah, denial. River in Egypt. Yada, yada, yada." Michelle returned the photo to her purse. "You just watch yourself, Miss High and Mighty. You always thought you were so much better than us. Well, Wade hasn't been around his kid for a while, and I'm guessing it's because he's been shacked up with you. When I tell him he'd gonna have to choose between his tramp and his son, which one do you think it'll be?" By the end of her rant, Michelle was flushed and breathing heavily.

Eva-Marie, on the other hand, had gone completely cold.

"I suppose we'll see, won't we?" she calmly told the other woman, then took a sip from her drink. "The band won't be on stage much longer. You're welcome to wait for Wade right here if you'd like. And just so you know, I never thought I was better than you. You did. That's why you didn't like me. I was friendly to everyone, but you and some of the others hated me on sight."

Cocking her head to the side, Eva-Marie eyed the other woman curiously.

"You know, that hasn't changed. I'm still nice to everyone." Giving Michelle a wry smile, she went on. "Lucky you. I can see you haven't changed either."

BJ strolled casually by.

"Hey, Eva-Marie. You okay?"

"I'm fine," she assured him.

Michelle huffed loudly again, grabbed her empty glass, and trotted off after a waitress.

"Who's your friend?" BJ asked.

"Correction, Wade's friend. Someone he knew in high school." So, BJ didn't know Michelle. Interesting.

After the set, Wade came back to Eva-Marie. He stood next to her, and held her close, while he conducted a couple of short interviews and signed a few autographs. She kept looking for Michelle to show up, but she was nowhere to be seen. Scott came by to give her a hug and a kiss on the cheek, before he sprinted away to catch up with a woman who'd caught his eye.

A few minutes later, Wade whispered to her that he was ready to leave. He sent a message to his friends, then his security detail whisked them through a side entrance, and to the limousine waiting for them there. During the ride back to her house, Wade wanted to kiss and cuddle, but Eva-Marie used the presence of the security team to put him off.

"They're in the front of the car, behind the partition, for shit's sake," Wade complained.

"They could still be watching. Or listening. You can't be too careful. I was raised by a diplomat, remember."

"Fine." He huffed, and she laughed in spite of her somber mood. "But you owe me, woman," he teased.

Back at her house, Wade was still in a playful mood, but Eva-Marie remained thoughtful and distracted. The truth was, she wasn't quite sure how to ask about Michelle without seeming jealous and nosy. She and Wade had a good thing, but at times, her place in his world wasn't concrete. Did she even have the right to question him about his personal affairs? Especially sensitive ones involving his exes and children? The diplomat's daughter felt she should smile and pretend everything was perfectly fine. The woman who loved Wade Davies wanted answers, and she wanted them now.

"Okay, what is it?" he asked, giving her just the opening she desired, but wasn't sure she should take.

"What is what?" she asked, feigning innocence and buying time to make a decision.

"You're too quiet. Something's on your mind. Spit it out," Wade demanded. His dark eyes bored into hers, drilling through her heart into her soul. She was talking before she realized it was happening.

"You told me you never married, yes?"

"Yes, that's what I told you." Wade frowned

at the question.

"Did you father any children?"

He looked shocked. Truly stunned, as if it was the last thing he expected to hear.

"No," he spoke slowly, as if he needed to take his time and make himself clear. "I don't have any kids. I've always been very careful, even when I was younger. I taught Scott to be the same way. When I have children, it will be with the woman I intend to spend my life with. Why are you asking me this?"

Now Eva-Marie was getting nervous. She could feel Wade's anger, and realized she'd made a huge mistake. But it was too late to turn back now. The only thing she could do was tell him why she'd gone down this road, and deal with the fallout.

"There was a woman in the club. Michelle. She was one of the girls you were with in high school, I believe. She had a picture of a child she said was your son. I didn't really believe her, of course, but he looked enough like you for it to be possible. She implied that you were neglecting the boy to be with me. That it was a pattern with you- a few hot and heavy weeks with a new fling, then on to the next one, and the child gets caught in the middle. I asked her to stay and talk to you herself, but she disappeared."

"Really." His voice was flatter than a balloon with no air. "Did she say anything else?"

"No, I think that was it."

Wade stood there, only a few feet away, but it felt like so many more. Even now, when he stared at her with such frosty fury, Eva-Marie's first thought was of how breathtakingly gorgeous he was, before she wondered how much of his anger was for Michelle, and how much she'd brought on herself. She didn't have to wait long to find out.

"So, you let Michelle get in your head and come between us." He folded his arms, and Eva-Marie immediately missed having access to them. "She made you believe you were just a fling I'm having while I'm at home. And that I have a child I neglect whenever I find some new pussy."

Wade ran his hand across the top of his head,

making his curls stand up in wild spikes. Then, closing his eyes and mouthing what looked like a prayer, he started to pace back and forth across the room. His face and posture were calmer, but his clenched fists gave away the fact that he was still extremely angry.

"I know we haven't been together that long, Em, but you've known me a long time. You've practically been a member of my family. You should be the first person to know when the things people say about me are lies."

"But I- "

Wade's hand came up, and Eva-Marie fell silent. He neither looked at her, nor broke his stride. She was hurt, and offended, but stayed quiet.

"In the past, whenever I was with someone, it was always aboveboard. No lies, and I never took advantage of anyone. I never asked for anything I couldn't give. Even a jailbird like me had some standards."

Eva-Marie flinched at the venom in his tone.

"Wade, I know you're angry with me," she

tried again.

"Angry is just the tip of the iceberg." He stalked close, finally standing almost nose to nose with her. Eva-Marie wasn't backing down. She would take whatever came.

"Yeah, I'm super pissed at Michelle for telling the lies in the first place. But you believed the, Em. You're my woman. You should know me better than that, but since you don't- I'd never lie to a woman to fuck her, nor would I ever need to; I'd never father a child with someone, then neglect my responsibilities; and I'd never neglect my kid to get up in any woman's cunt. *What kind of bastard do you think I am, Eva-Marie?*"

The last of it was yelled directly in her face. By then, her tears were flowing so fast, she could barely see the look of disgust on his face before he turned and strode away. The door slammed behind him hard enough to rattle all the windows in her house. Knowing in her heart he was gone for good, Eva-Marie sank down to the carpet, laying her head on the sofa, crying until she was spent.

****

Wade was over being mad at Eva-Marie before he'd made it halfway home. He was still pissed off, just not at her. Now that he'd taken a few deep breaths and thought about it, Em was the only innocent in the whole shit show that went down tonight. He wanted to turn around and go back to her, and try to apologize. But after the way he'd behaved, she'd probably kick his ass and leave one of her high heels inside as a parting gift.

And she'd be justified. He'd been in her face about how long and how well she should know him, and how she was almost a part of his family, when only half of that was true. His family loved her, and they'd been acquainted for many years. But she barely knew him. He'd held himself apart from her, only growling a greeting here and there. Being a smartass every time she'd tried to be friendly toward him. Watching from the shadows like a lovesick fool as she smiled and laughed with his brother.

Now, when she was finally his, the first thing

he'd done was let her down. In fact, he'd done all the things he was sure her parents were still afraid of. He'd brought drama, negative media attention, and association with people of dubious character into her life. Wade almost laughed out loud, clearly hearing Mr. Robinson's voice in his head enunciating each terrible offence. The ambassador like to pretend the slightest variation from his plans meant the end of the world. Eva-Marie had always given her dad a little hell in her own way. He smiled. His Em was a firecracker.

His Em. Hopefully, she still was. If he hadn't completely fucked that up. He would see tomorrow. There were a couple of things he had to do first.

****

Wade got a little satisfaction from the startled guilt on Michelle's face when she saw him. He'd found out where she worked, and was sitting on his car in the parking lot when she walked out, casually signing a few autographs and posing for pictures. Excusing himself from the fans, he

117

greeted Michelle warmly before reclaiming his seat on the hood of the car.

"So, where's this kid of mine I've heard so much about?" he asked, getting right to the point. "Do I get to meet him, or what? I mean, it's not my fault I'm a deadbeat dad if I don't know the boy exists, right?"

Michelle's face flushed a splotchy red. With a white-knuckled grip on her purse, she made a dash for her car, but Wade moved faster and blocked her door. He was careful not to touch her, but thought he saw her flinch anyway. Holding up both hands, palms forward, he indicated he meant her no harm.

"I just want to know why you did it, Michelle. Are you still mad that I turned you down in high school?"

She looked at Wade like he'd read her diary, so horrified, exposed, and vulnerable. Then came the anger. She dug around in her purse, and came up with a small cannister of pepper spray, aiming it at Wade.

"No, you asshole. It wasn't about that. So,

you weren't interested in me in high school. Big deal. You fucked half the school anyway. They were whores. I was pretty. Sexy. Classy."

"Girls who beg for dick aren't classy."

"You bastard." She waved the little spray can threateningly.

"If you want to add an assault charge to the list of things I'm about to tell you, go ahead." Wade waited, trying to appear calm, hoping his words would sink in before Michelle sent him to the emergency room.

"What do you mean?" She backed up, looking nervous. "What things?"

"I know exactly who the father of your son is." At Michelle's stricken grimace, Wade continued. "My lawyer has a copy of Steve's and your marriage license and your son's birth certificate. If the question of my being your son's father ever comes up again, the documents will be made public, and I'll demand a paternity test."

"No," Michelle pleaded, "please don't do that to my son."

"I didn't bring him into this, you did," Wade

persisted. "Look, I'm certain Jeremy and Steve were the ones who put you up to telling Eva-Marie the lie. The thing is, I don't know what their problem is. I've never done anything to either of them. I kept them from getting their asses kicked, and I even went to jail for something I didn't do because Jeremy's father had weird fixation on me."

Michelle's wry smile caught him off guard.

"Those guys were always so jealous of you they could barely see straight. You were cool and gorgeous. You got all the girls. You had that badass car you still have. And you never got caught doing anything, but those dopes always did. Plus, your brother was already a rock star before he even graduated high school. Everybody knew you could have been one too back then, but you didn't even care."

"What?" Wade was stunned.

"Oh, yeah," Michelle giggled. "I think Jeremy bitched about you being perfect so much, even his dad started to hate you."

Wade was struck completely dumb for a few

seconds. A year and a half in jail, and years of putting up with craziness from his former friends, and it was all because of immaturity and jealousy? There had to be some other reason, but Wade couldn't think of a single one. What a fucking waste. The absurdity of it all made him laugh out loud.

"Michelle," his smile was broad and genuine, "tell you husband and his friends to grow the fuck up and stay out of my life. If I have to say it again, it will involve lawyers and reporters. Ask them if they really want the world knowing all their business. That tends to happen to people around me. And if there's any question about it, I've got nothing to lose. I didn't do anything but get railroaded by a dirty cop."

At the words *dirty cop*, Michelle flinched again. Wade eyed her closely, then moved away from her car door.

"Hey, Michelle, I don't know what's going on, and I won't ask," he spoke reassuringly, "but if you and your son ever need to get out of a bad situation, you can come to the garage and I'll help you out. Or you can contact Eva-Marie at the Robinson Foundation if I'm not here. She'll help you."

She stared at him, as if gauging his sincerity.

"Why would you help me? And especially her. Why would she do anything for me?"

"Because Eva-Marie is a genuinely good person, Michelle. She truly is. And believe it or not, I'm a good guy, too. Hopefully, good enough to deserve her. But, either way, we'll take care of you if you need help. Your boy deserves a happy home."

Walking back to his car, he called back to her, "It was good seeing you again. Sorry it had to be like this."

Driving away, Wade felt as if a huge weight had been lifted.

****

Eva-Marie wasn't answering any of his phone calls. He couldn't reach her at home, or at her office. He knew it was Sunday, but he'd tried her there anyway, knowing she went in on weekends sometimes. Nothing. She was probably mad as hell at him. He didn't blame her. But he couldn't beg her forgiveness if he couldn't find her.

After leaving several messages, he gave up and went down to the shop. He raised the bay doors to half mast, then cranked up the music and started working on a car.

It scared the crap out of Wade when he felt his body being yanked from beneath the car. The ratchet he held clattered to the floor, barely missing his head. He raised his hands, fully ready to throw a punch, but the culprit who grabbed him by the wrists and straddled his chest was Eva-Marie.

Wade tried to embrace her, but she wasn't having it.

"I've been looking for you all day," he told her. She didn't seem to hear him. Instead, she took a deep breath and closed her eyes.

"I have something to say," she blurted out. "I'll make it fast, so you can get back to work."

"Em," he started again. This time she reached down with her free hand and covered his mouth.

"It will be even quicker if you just let me get it over with and don't interrupt. Please."

The sadness in her eyes cut him deeply. He lay still and quiet, no longer certain whether the damage he'd done was fixable or not. When Eva-Marie stood, Wade immediately missed the weight and warmth of her body on his. The thought of never lying beneath her again, seeing her eyes filled with love as she rose above him, hurt to his soul. She loved him, he realized now, though she'd never actually said the words.

"I thought about what you said. Almost non-stop, to be honest. You talked about how well we should know each other. Well, you're right. We *should* know each other better. But maybe I'm not the only one with a problem in that area. You accused me of believing Michelle's lies about you. Screamed in my face without letting me say a word to defend myself. And since you walked out, I'm assuming you don't want to hear this, but it needs to be said anyway."

Bending down, she poked him in the chest to

124

emphasize each syllable.

"*I never said I believed Michelle.*"

Wade grabbed the spot on his chest. Shit. Eva-Marie poked him hard as hell. He was likely to have a bruise, mad as she was. He'd never seen her like this. Fuck, he was probably going to get dumped.

Straightening up again, she continued.

"I only repeated what she said, which is what you asked me to do. By now, I think every woman in the world has been made aware of your pattern with women. You're the love'em and leave'em kind. It wasn't news when she told me that, either, Wade. I knew this wasn't just a fling, but I also knew it wasn't permanent. However, the only thing I asked was if you were the father of her son. I told you I didn't thinks so, but the boy looked so much like you I couldn't be sure. And I remember Michelle hanging around you back then. She used to be all over you all the time."

Eva-Marie grimaced, and Wade thought about how cute she was when she wrinkled her nose like that. Also, how determined and final her expression was. His belly flipped over.

She blew out a tired-sounding sigh.

"Anyway, I want you to know I don't think you're a bastard. Quite the opposite. I've always thought you were a great guy. This isn't going to work, though. I'm sorry. I guess we really are too different. Goodbye, Wade."

She turned quickly and ducked under the door. It was like she couldn't wait to get away from him. It wasn't pleasant, having the tables turned this way. Eva-Marie might leave him, but he had things of his own to say before she left. Vaulting to his feet, he sprinted after her.

"Eva-Marie!"

She wasn't stopping. In fact, she might have sped up when she heard him call her name.

"Em. Come on. Stop. I need to talk to you. Wait a damn minute, Em. Please."

He had one hand on the car door and one hand on her arm. He could feel her stiffen in his grasp before going limp and allowing him to maneuver her body into a position where she couldn't escape. Eva-Marie did not look happy about it. Not one little bit.

"Em, honey, I've been looking for you all over so I could apologize."

She turned away and refused to look at him. Disappointed, Wade slid his hands down her arms to grasp her hands, and continued to be as sincere as he knew how to be.

"I mean it, Em. I must have called you a dozen times. I drove to your home, your office, and even to a couple of the places you hang out. To tell you the truth, I feel like a fucking stalker."

Still no reaction. This was bad. It didn't matter. He was prepared to do as much heavy duty groveling as it took. Losing Eva-Marie was not an option.

"Look, baby," Wade squeezed her hands, and she finally lifted her tear-filled gaze to his. Oh, hell, she was crying, and it was all his fault. The princess should never shed tears over a nobody like him. He definitely didn't deserve them. Maybe she was right to cut her losses and run. He would probably serve her better by letting her, though it would kill him to do it.

"I'm really sorry, okay? As soon as I calmed down, I realized none of it was your fault, and you were being used to get back at me. I overreacted." Wade panicked when Eva-Marie pulled one of her hands away. But it was only to wipe at her tears. Pulling a clean towel from his pocket, he gently dabbed at them himself. Damn, he loved this woman. Losing her would break him like nothing else had.

"Thank you," she said, her voice barely above a whisper. Always the polite princess. "I was mad, but you scared me, too. I've never seen you freak out like that."

"I went off because it's important to me how you see me. You're my princess." Wade stroked a finger across the softness of her cheek, and dragged his thumb along her plump bottom lip, hoping he'd get to kiss it again. "I know I'll never be worthy of you, but I wanted to be more than just a jailbird or grease monkey love'em and leave'em guy from high school to you."

Wade brought Eva-Marie's hand he still held

to his lips and kissed it. He tried to release her and walk away, but she stubbornly held on to him.

"I'm no princess." She gave a harsh sounding laugh. "And you're no jailbird," she snapped at Wade. "We both know you were innocent."

She was irritated with him. The Canberra in her accent was thick, and her golden eyes flashed like those of an ancient goddess.

"How dare you think I'm so shallow, as if I was just some society girl who wanted to go slumming. For your information, Wade Davies, you're not a grease monkey to me. You're a businessman, and an entrepreneur. A pioneer. A brand. You're a fucking rock star." Eva-Marie moved in closer, cradling Wade's face in her hands. He could see the sincerity in her eyes. Could practically see straight through to her soul.

"You're my friend, my lover," Eva-Marie continued, while Wade's heart pounded hard enough to beat right out of his chest. "The sexiest damned man on the planet, and the only man I've ever loved. But every time I think you're mine, something happens to mess it up."

"You love me," Wade repeated, happy for the confirmation. "I love you, too."

Gathering Eva-Marie close, he simply held her. Never again would he take for granted how amazing it was to have her in his arms.

"I'm yours, Em. And you're mine. Nothing is going to change that, I promise," he whispered into her russet curls. "Let's stick together from now on. I'm never letting you go."

"Good," she spoke against his chest. "Sticking together is good."

Chuckling, Wade leaned in to seal their new bond with a kiss, which quickly turned passionate. His hands roamed every familiar curve of Eva-Marie's body with new appreciation. Her answering caresses were just as wickedly hot as his, touching him everywhere she could reach, and making him wish for so much more.

"We need to take this inside unless you want to give all the neighbors a show."

Startled, she tried to pull away from him, but

Wade held her tight. He'd be hanging on to her from now on.

"Come on." He drew her alongside him toward the bay doors."

"Hey, will that rolling thing you were lying on support us?" Eva-Marie wanted to know.

"The creeper? Ooh, you dirty girl," Wade teased, swatting her on the butt.

Eva-Marie blushed, still waiting for an answer.

"No, unfortunately, I don't think so. But, I'll reinforce one just for us to play with. I'll do it tomorrow."

She giggled, a sound Wade was glad to hear. Keeping Eva-Marie happy was his main goal in the future. After locking down the garage, he took her upstairs and sat on the sofa, pulling her onto his lap.

"Are you sure, Em, that being with me is enough for you?"

"Yes, baby," she answered without hesitation. "I love you. I always have. You're all I need."

Wrapping his arms around her, Wade

repeated, "I love you, too, Em. You're my world."

"Show me," she challenged.

Of course, he complied.

"Gladly."

Sealing his lips to hers, Wade kissed Eva-Marie, trying to make her forget everything except how much she was adored.

THE END

CHANDRA CRAWFORD

ACKNOWLEDGEMENTS

Thanks as always to Sassie and Willsin, both are genius at what they do. They provide me with unending mentoring and guidance. I love them the mostest.

All my love to Benjamin, Genia, Nina, Chad, and Marie, the best support system ever.
And special thanks go out to model Kenolivier Gisbert for bringing life to Wade.

CHANDRA CRAWFORD

ABOUT THE AUTHOR

Chandra Crawford has been an avid reader since she learned the alphabet at age 3. She enjoys almost any type of fiction, and has always dreamed of being a writer. A hopeless romantic herself, her characters tend to lead her in that direction.

Her stories are like cotton candy- hot, sweet fluff that melts in your mouth and leaves you happy. Romance with a heavy dose of smut, designed to entertain, titillate, and inspire some naughty fun.

Completely in love with book boyfriends, Chandra is currently in search of her own billionaire cowboy exNavy SEAL sugar daddy to be her submissive.

www.ChandraFaimas.weebly.com